DRAGON PAINTER

by Adam Bushnell and Amerigo Pinelli

FRANKLIN WATTS
LONDON·SYDNEY

Once upon a time, there was

a rich and powerful emperor.

But the Emperor had a problem.

Pigeons had made nests on the roof

of his palace. They made such a noise!

They cooed and cooed and cooed

from morning until night.

So, the Emperor sent for a painter –

the best painter in the world.

When the painter arrived,

the Emperor asked him to climb

on to the roof and paint pictures of eagles.

The Emperor thought that the pictures

would scare away the pigeons.

The painter climbed on to the roof.

He painted huge and scary eagles.

They had sharp beaks and deadly claws.

The pigeons were frightened.

They flew away and never returned.

The Emperor was delighted.
He invited the painter inside
to see his palace.

"I have a beautiful palace, but look –
my walls are bare," said the Emperor.
"I love dragons. I want you to paint
huge and colourful dragons
on these three walls."

The painter began to work straight away.

First, he painted a red dragon breathing fire.

Next, he painted a blue dragon breathing ice.

Finally, he painted a yellow dragon

breathing smoke.

8

9

The Emperor clapped his hands with joy.

But then he stopped and peered closely

at the dragons. He pointed at the eyes.

"Why haven't you coloured in their eyes?"

he asked.

"Oh, your highness, I can never colour in

the eyes of a dragon!" the painter replied.

"Why not?" asked the Emperor.

"If I colour in the eyes, then the dragon will

come to life," the painter said firmly.

The Emperor roared with laughter.

"Don't be so silly," he said.

"Colour in the eyes of the dragons!"

But the painter shook his head.

"No."

"Colour in the eyes, right now!"

the Emperor commanded,

stamping his feet.

Again the painter said, "No."

"Do it now!" the Emperor ordered,

shaking his fist at the painter.

But again the painter refused.

"No," he said, "I can never colour in

the eyes of a dragon. Not ever!"

"Right," the Emperor said angrily,

"I'll colour in the eyes myself!"

He took a paintbrush and coloured in

the eyes of each dragon.

Suddenly, there was a loud rumbling sound.

The red dragon, the blue dragon

and the yellow dragon all came to life.

Each dragon peeled itself off the wall.

Each dragon roared.

The red dragon blew fire.

The blue dragon blew ice.

The yellow dragon blew smoke.

The dragons flew up high. They smashed a hole

in the roof of the palace. Away into the sky

they went. The dragons burnt buildings,

froze farms and blew smoke all over the land.

The Emperor looked at the painter.

"You were right!" he gasped.

"We must make sure that this

will never happen again."

The painter nodded.

"I wish you had listened to me," he sighed.

The Emperor decided to make a new law.
No one in the land should ever colour in
the eyes of a dragon. And this is still a tradition
in China to this very day.

Story order

Look at these 5 pictures and captions.
Put the pictures in the right order
to retell the story.

1

The dragons flew across the land.

2

The Emperor painted in the dragons' eyes.

3

The Emperor asked for painted dragons.

4

The painter refused to paint the eyes.

5

The dragons peeled off the walls.

Independent Reading

This series is designed to provide an opportunity for your child to read on their own. These notes are written for you to help your child choose a book and to read it independently.

In school, your child's teacher will often be using reading books which have been banded to support the process of learning to read. Use the book band colour your child is reading in school to help you make a good choice. *Dragon Painter* is a good choice for children reading at Gold Band in their classroom to read independently.

The aim of independent reading is to read this book with ease, so that your child enjoys the story and relates it to their own experiences.

About the book

Dragon Painter tells the story behind the Chinese traditional eye-dotting ceremony. The Emperor refuses to allow the painter to leave the dragons' eyes blank, but by painting them, he brings the dragons to life.

Before reading

Help your child to learn how to make good choices by asking: "Why did you choose this book? Why do you think you will enjoy it?" Look at the cover together and ask: "What do you think the story will be about?" Ask your child to think of what they already know about dragons in Chinese culture. Discuss that they are important creatures in China and that there is a dragon dance to celebrate Lunar New Year. Then ask your child to read the title aloud. Ask: "Do you think the story will be about real or painted dragons?" Remind your child that they can sound out the letters to make a word if they get stuck. Decide together whether your child will read the story independently or read it aloud to you.

During reading

Remind your child of what they know and what they can do independently. If reading aloud, support your child if they hesitate or ask for help by telling the word. If reading to themselves, remind your child that they can come and ask for your help if stuck.

After reading

Support comprehension by asking your child to tell you about the story. Use the story order puzzle to encourage your child to retell the story in the right sequence, in their own words. The correct sequence can be found on the next page.

Help your child think about the messages in the book that go beyond the story and ask: "Why do you think the Emperor did not believe the painter? Do you think the painter was brave to stand up to the Emperor? What lesson do you think the Emperor might have learned?" Give your child a chance to respond to the story: "Have you ever not been believed about something? What happened?"

Extending learning

Help your child predict other possible outcomes of the story by asking: "Do you think that the Emperor still loves dragons? Why/why not? Do you think the painter will paint more dragons? Do you think he might do anything differently next time?"

In the classroom, your child's teacher may be teaching contractions. There are many examples in this book that you could look at together, including *I'll* (I will), *haven't* (have not), *don't* (do not).

Find these together and point out how the apostrophes are used in place of the omitted letters.

Franklin Watts
First published in Great Britain in 2020
by The Watts Publishing Group

Copyright © The Watts Publishing Group 2020
All rights reserved.

Series Editors: Jackie Hamley and Melanie Palmer
Series Advisors: Dr Sue Bodman and Glen Franklin
Series Designers: Peter Scoulding and Cathryn Gilbert

A CIP catalogue record for this book is
available from the British Library.

ISBN 978 1 4451 7177 7 (hbk)
ISBN 978 1 4451 7178 4 (pbk)
ISBN 978 1 4451 7312 2 (library ebook)

Printed in China

Franklin Watts
An imprint of
Hachette Children's Group
Part of The Watts Publishing Group
Carmelite House
50 Victoria Embankment
London EC4Y 0DZ

An Hachette UK Company
www.hachette.co.uk

www.reading-champion.co.uk

FSC
www.fsc.org
MIX
Paper from
responsible sources
FSC® C104740

Answer to Story order: 3, 4, 2, 5, 1